PUSS IN BOOTS

A GOOD KITTY AND A BAD EGG

adapted by Ilanit Oliver
illustrated by Brigette Barrager

Ready-to-Read

Simon Spotlight

New York   London   Toronto   Sydney   New Delhi

SIMON SPOTLIGHT
An imprint of Simon & Schuster Children's Publishing Division
1230 Avenue of the Americas, New York, New York 10020
Puss In Boots ® & © 2011 DreamWorks Animation L.L.C.
All rights reserved, including the right of reproduction in whole or in part in any form.
SIMON SPOTLIGHT, READY-TO-READ, and colophon are registered trademarks of Simon & Schuster, Inc.
For information about special discounts for bulk purchases, please contact
Simon & Schuster Special Sales at 1-866-506-1949 or business@simonandschuster.com.
Manufactured in the United States of America 0911 LAK
First Edition
2 4 6 8 10 9 7 5 3 1
ISBN 978-1-4424-2891-1
ISBN 978-1-4424-3938-2 (eBook)

Before Puss In Boots was a legend, he was just Puss—a good kitty who was friends with a bad egg named Humpty Alexander Dumpty.

The story of Puss In Boots
and Humpty Dumpty
goes back many years.
It all began in the town of
San Ricardo.

One day a basket holding
a tiny kitty blew onto the steps
of an orphanage.
The owner of the orphanage
was named Imelda.
She was very kind
and gave the kitty a home.

At dinner that night
Little Boy Blue teased Puss.
Humpty Dumpty told the boy
to pick on someone his own size!

"Who asked you?" said Little Boy Blue. "Let's spin him!" "Please don't!" yelled Humpty, but Little Boy Blue did not listen. So Puss used his spoon to defend Humpty from Little Boy Blue!

Humpty told Puss that he was
looking for magic beans.
"The magic beans will grow
into a beanstalk so tall it
will reach a castle in the clouds!"
he said.

"Inside the castle there is a
Giant and a Golden Goose.
One of her golden eggs could
set me up for life!" he added.
Puss loved listening to Humpty speak
of legends and adventures.

The two boys grew close.
Puss began to share Humpty's
dream of finding the magic beans.
The boys formed the Bean Club.
"From this day forth," they vowed,
"It shall be known, never alone,
always together. Humpty and
Puss, brothers forever."

When they got older, the boys
looked for trouble . . . and found it!
They played tricks and stole
beans from the market.
Humpty had the brains.
Puss had the skill.
Humpty's plans were not
always honest, but they worked.

The boys took the stolen beans
and planted them in the garden.
Maybe this time they would
grow into the magic beanstalk!

"You never know when you are going to get lucky," said Humpty.

But one day, something changed
their friendship forever. . . .
The brothers were throwing rocks
off a rooftop when one hit a
carriage and knocked open the door.
Out charged a bull!

It raced toward an old woman.
Puss acted fast! He jumped off the
roof and slid down a clothesline,
pulling the woman out of the way.
The old woman was the
Comandante's mother,
and Puss became a hero!

For his bravery, Imelda gave Puss
a pair of boots, a belt, and a hat
fit for a hero.
Puss tried to live up to the honor.
"I am not stealing anymore, Humpty,"
Puss told his friend.

"But we're partners," Humpty pleaded.
"We are brothers," Puss said.
"And that will never change."
But the brothers grew apart.

Then one night Humpty woke Puss.
Humpty said a group of people
was chasing him.
But Humpty was lying!
Instead, he tricked Puss
into helping him steal gold
from the San Ricardo Bank.

"You tricked me!" Puss cried.
"I had to!" Humpty replied.
"You left me no choice!"

Soon the police were chasing them.
Humpty drove the carriage
across the bridge, but he was going
too fast and lost control.
Humpty and Puss flew out.
The carriage plunged into the river.
The gold was gone forever.

Humpty had fallen and he could not
get up.
"Puss, help me!" Humpty pleaded.
"Save yourself," Puss replied as he
dove off the bridge and into the
water.

Each brother felt betrayed
by the other. Without Puss's help,
Humpty was caught by the police
and sent to jail.

Because of Humpty, Puss lost his
honor, his home, and his brother.
Since then, he had been searching
for a way to repay the town
of San Ricardo.

Then one day, years later, Puss met Humpty again. Humpty said he finally knew how to get the magic beans. He and his partner, Kitty Softpaws, needed Puss's help. "What do you say? Partners?" Humpty asked hopefully.

"No. Never again," Puss replied.
But Humpty was convincing.
"All I am asking for is a second
chance. Give me that, and I will
help you pay back San Ricardo,
and everyone will forgive you."
"I will do this for San Ricardo,"
Puss announced.

So they began the plan.
They stole the beans from
Jack and Jill, planted them,
and found the castle.
They also found the Golden Goose,
and captured her!

They climbed back down the vine
and made it to safety. They did it!
"I never wanted to be an outlaw,"
Puss told Humpty. "All I ever
wanted was to go home.
Now I finally can, thanks to you."

The next morning, Puss awoke to find
Humpty, Kitty, and the Goose gone!
Humpty had betrayed Puss again.
Humpty had taken the Golden Goose
to San Ricardo so he would look like
a hero instead of Puss. He offered
everyone golden eggs.

Then Puss was caught for helping rob the bank.
Humpty did not realize that the Golden Goose's mother, the Great Terror, was coming to get her child back.
"The town will be in danger!" yelled Puss.

Soon the Great Terror arrived.
Humpty realized that he had
made a big mistake and led
her out of town. But Humpty's
carriage crashed. He and the
Golden Goose fell over the side
of the bridge!

Puss tried to save them.

"I will not leave you behind, Humpty," Puss assured him.

But Humpty began to slip!

He didn't want to make Puss choose between saving him and saving the Golden Goose, so he let go of the rope and fell.

When he landed, Humpty cracked his shell. He was solid gold inside!

"I'm a golden egg!" he cheered. Finally, Puss gave the Golden Goose back to her mother.

And even though they went their separate ways, Humpty and Puss knew that they would be brothers forever.